DATE DUE

NOV 04

GAYLORD			PRINTED IN U.S.A.

Break-up

FACING UP To Divorce

Gianni Padoan   Illustrated by Emanuela Collini

Published by Child's Play (International) Ltd
Swindon   **Bologna**   **New York**
© 1987 Happy Books Milan Italy   ISBN 0-85953-310-7   Printed in Singapore
English La̶n̶g̶u̶a̶g̶e̶ Edition © Child's Play (International) Limited
This impr̶

FACING UP SERIES

Other titles

Remembering Grandad

Danger Kid

Follow my Leader

Normally, I can't get away
from school quickly enough,
but there I was at 3.30
trying to keep everyone behind
by showing them my stamp album.
"... and that one's from Italy, and
this one was on a letter my uncle
sent from Nigeria ..."

But gradually everyone started
to drift away. I tried to persuade
Gwen to come home for tea.
"Sorry, Joe. I promised Clare
I'd go back to her house today.
How about tomorrow?"
"O.K." I said in my best "no-it's-
not-o.k." voice. But it didn't work.

Still, at least I could depend
on James. We walked together
to the end of my street,
and I began to cheer up.
"Er, James?" I tried to sound
as though it didn't matter.
"Coming for tea?"

"Sorry, Joe," said James. "We're visiting my Grandma. I promised Mum I'd be back by four. I'd better run!" And he did.
I choked back my tears, kicked a coke tin into the road, and thought about last night.

It had been late, but I hadn't been able to sleep. I'd come downstairs in my pyjamas to fetch a glass of water. Mum and Dad were shouting at each other again, like they'd been doing all the time recently. Mum was crying, and Dad sounded near tears. I stood there, the tears trickling down my face, and listened. I didn't understand half of it, but it sounded pretty bad.

I walked up our street as slowly as
I could, but finally I couldn't put off
going into the house any longer.
As I pushed open the front door,
a furry express train jumped up
and licked several layers of skin
off my face.
"Down, Rufus!" I yelled. And then,
more quietly, "Mum? Where are you?"

She was in the kitchen, cooking
dinner, and I could tell from the way
she looked that something
was wrong.
"Sit down, love," she said.
"We need to talk."

I knew then that something
was really wrong. It was years
since she had spoken to me
like that.
"Is it about you and Dad arguing?"
I blurted out. "Mum, I've been
thinking. I'll do extra housework,
if it helps. I'll do anything . . .
I'll even take less pocket money."
Mum smiled sadly. "It's not
your fault, Joe," she said.
"Please, Mum," I begged.
"Please . . . are you going to stop
fighting soon?"
Mum went very quiet and pale.
"Yes, love," she said. "We are.
Very soon. Dad's moving out."

It was as though it had been
staring me in the face for years,
but I'd been too stupid to
recognise it. I thought something
like that could never happen to us.
We didn't have problems like that.
I didn't know what to say.
I swallowed hard. "When?" I asked.
Mum looked down at her hands.
"Tomorrow," she said.
All of a sudden there was a huge lump
in my throat and tears pushing
from behind my eyes.
"No!" I shouted. "I don't want you
to! I hate you both!"
Throwing up my arm to hide the tears,
I dashed from the room.

"Joe!" called my Mum. "Joe! Come back!"
Her voice sounded as though she was stranded in the middle of the desert with only vultures for company. But I couldn't help her.
Not now, not yet.
I ran upstairs to my room, and threw myself on the bed. I howled and howled like I used to when I was a kid. All I could think of was how Mum and Dad must hate me. If they liked me even the littlest bit, they would never have hurt me like this. Just as I was feeling like the last person left on a dead star in a dying universe, Rufus came in, pushed his wet nose into my hand, and flopped down on the floor by my bed.
I had calmed down by the time Dad came home from work, and said yes when he offered to take me to the zoo for an hour before it closed.
As we walked round the cages, I held tightly onto his hand, to show him that I didn't want him to go.
I knew if I tried to say it in words, I wouldn't be able to keep from crying.
We stopped in front of the monkey cage, and laughed as they swung and jumped around. All of a sudden, some of the monkeys started fighting, scratching and biting each other, while the others dived out of the way. I managed a joke. "Just like home," I said, with a weak smile.

Dad smiled too, and we walked on.
"It's true though," he said.
"Sometimes a home gets to be like
a cage. You feel shut in, as though
there's no escape. And so you take
it out on the others."
"Is that why you hate me and Mum?"
"I don't, son. But your Mum and I can't
get on. We don't agree. We don't love
each other any more. We don't know
why things have changed. But they have.
The important thing is that we both
love you as much as we ever did.
We'll both go on loving you."

I nodded, but I wasn't sure it made
sense. How could he love me if he
wasn't living in the same house?

That night I had a weird dream.
I was being tossed about in a rough
sea, but the more I tried to swim,
the more I sank under each huge
wave. I was shouting for someone
to come and pull me out, but the only
people I could see were Mum
and Dad. They were floating
in the sky, but away from each
other – and away from me.

The next day was the very worst day in my whole life. All I could think about was my Dad walking out on us. Never again would he live in our house. Never again would I jump on his bed to wake him in the morning, never help him wash the car, or bake bread, like we used to.

I began to dream of ways to bring him back. Suppose I had an accident? What if I just grew ill with worry? Then the teachers would ring home. Mum and Dad would come to school, arm in arm, and tell me what an awful mistake they'd made. They hadn't realised how this was hurting me, and they'd decided to stick together after all.
But deep inside, I realised that this wasn't going to happen.

Gwen and James found me propped against a wall at break.
"Joe?" said Gwen. "What's the matter? What's wrong? Why are you looking so sad?"
I told them what was happening. How Dad was leaving. How Mum agreed it was the best thing. How they didn't love me any more.

"Of course they do," said Gwen. "Don't you remember when my little brother was born? My parents spent so much time with him that I was sure they had forgotten all about me."

"Anyway, people don't need to be around *all* the time," said James. "I missed my Grandad a lot when he first died, but now it's like he's around whenever I think of him. And you're lucky. Even if you're not living with him, you'll still be seeing your Dad."

They stayed with me all break and all lunch time, and we walked home together after school. By the time we reached our house I was almost cheerful.

But as soon as I walked in through the front door it all came back to me. The house was quiet. Even Rufus didn't bark when I opened the door. I went upstairs. There was Dad packing his cases – and Mum was helping him!

I wanted to say to her, "Whose side are you on?" I wanted to stop him going. But deep down I knew it was too late.

The days that followed were sad.
I went to school and I still went
to the park. But I didn't want to do
anything. Nothing interested me,
not even bike racing in the park.
James and Gwen gave up trying
to cheer me up.

When my Dad had left, he said
he would see me at the weekend,
but I just couldn't wait that long.
I phoned him at his office.
"Dad?" I said. "It's me. I miss
you." I couldn't think what
else to say. But he understood.
"Wait for me. I'll be there
in a few minutes," he said.

We went to a terrific snack bar.
I had three Big Macs with fries,
two milk shakes and one jumbo
knickerbocker glory.
"Are you in training for
the Fattest Boy in the World
competition?" joked Dad.
"I haven't felt much like eating
lately," I replied. "But I'm hungry
now. I could eat a horse!"

We sat there and talked for ages,
more than I could ever remember
us doing. Dad seemed much happier.
Maybe he wasn't worrying so much.
It was almost as good as having
him back. When he took me home,
I was already looking forward
to the weekend.

Mum was the same. She began spending more time talking to me instead of staring out of the window. She seemed more like her old self. I helped her more than I used to with things like cleaning, washing and shopping, but it was fun. We laughed more.

At the weekend, Dad took me shopping to buy me some new football kit. It was the day before the last match of the season, and I was starting to feel nervous and excited.

On the day of the match, though,
I felt different. I couldn't join in
with the joking in the changing
room. I couldn't help thinking
that the last time I had played,
Mum and Dad had come to watch
together, and had held hands and
laughed as they cheered me on.
All that was over now. I wasn't
even sure that Dad would be there.
Would he argue with Mum if he did
turn up? Would he stand with her?
I felt like running out of
the changing room and never
playing football again. But before
I could, the trainer came into
the room.
"Come on lads!" he shouted.
"Let's show them!"
We all trooped onto the field,
and I looked around anxiously
to see who was there.

The first two people I saw
in the crowd were Gwen and James.
Those two would never let me down.
Then I heard someone shouting
my name.
"Joe! Joe! Over here!" It was my Dad.
He was with Anne. I'd met her
a couple of times before, and
she seemed really nice.
"Come and have a pizza with us
afterwards!" shouted Dad.
"Great!" I called. "See you later!"
Then I saw Mum. She was with her
friend Mark. He was taking us
to the seaside tomorrow.
"Come on, Joe!" she yelled. "Hit
the back of the net!"
As the game got under way, I felt
as though I had my own personal
fan club. Maybe Mum and Dad
wouldn't ever get together again.
But if they were happy, and still
loved me, perhaps I was luckier
than some kids who had both parents
at home.

Oh, I nearly forgot! I scored a
brilliant goal, and we won the cup!